MacKenzie Smiles, LLC
San Francisco, CA

www.mackenziesmiles.com

Originally published as *Når to skal stå opp*
Copyright © Gyldendal Norsk Forlag AS 2002 [All rights reserved]
www.gyldendal.no

Original text by Tor Age Bringsvaerd
Original illustrations by Tina Soli

Translated by Tonje Vetleseter

Art production by Bernard Prinz

ISBN 9780981576145

Printed in China

10 9 8 7 6 5 4 3 2 1

Distributed in the U.S. and Canada by:
Ingram Publisher Services
One Ingram Blvd.
P.O. Box 3006
LaVergne, TN 37086
(888) 800-5978

Tor Age Bringsvaerd

when two get up

Illustrated by Tina Soli

Translated by Tonje Vetleseter

MACKENZIE
SMILES
San Francisco

When two **dragons** get up...

...they **yawn** so **big** they **hit** their **teeth** on the **ceiling!**

When two
rhinos
get up...

when two bananas get up...

When two slippers get up...

When two **trolls**
get up...

...they carefully **peek** under the **shades** and **hope** the sun **isn't** shining.

...they **start** their day with a **song** and a **dance.**

when two **elephants** get up...

...they **stomp** around and **scream,** "Where are my trousers?"

When two **pillows**
get up...

...they **pat** each other's **stomach** and smooth out all **their wrinkles.**

When two **newspapers** get **up**...

...they **scare** each **other** with **big, bold** letters.

when **Daddy** and I _get up..._

Then we **finish** getting **dressed**...

...and eat **breakfast** together.

Kitty gets breakfast, too!

Afterward, **Daddy** takes **me**

to school!